For John & Milo,
Maddy & Harry
and Elizabeth Hawkins

Many thanks
Eileen

For Amy J.C.

First published in Great Britain in 2009
by Piccadilly Press Ltd,
5 Castle Road, London NW1 8PR
www.piccadillypress.co.uk

Designed by Simon Davis
Printed and bound by WKT in China
Colour reproduction by Dot Gradations

ISBN: 978 1 84812 004 4 (paperback)
ISBN: 978 1 84812 005 1 (hardback)

1 3 5 7 9 10 8 6 4 2

A catalogue record of this book is available from the British Library

Where's The Bus?

Eileen Browne • James Croft

Piccadilly Press • London

"Duck has asked us to
tea," said Rabbit.
"Yippity, hippity, hop!
I love going to tea."

"It's too far to walk,"
said Mouse.
"We'll get the bus."

They hopped and scurried to the bus stop.

"Where's our bus?" said Mouse.
"I'm hungry NOW."

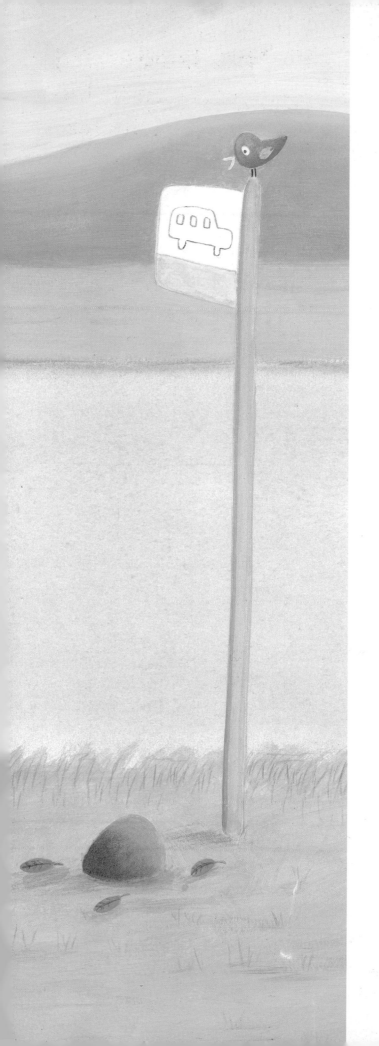

"I can smell something,"
said Rabbit, sniffing the air.
"Strawberries!
Scrum diddly-dum!"
She skipped away from
the bus stop.

"We might miss the bus,"
called Mouse.
"Mind you, I could eat a
strawberry or two myself."

Rabbit and Mouse

ate some strawberries.

Then they went back
to the bus stop.
"Where's our bus?"
said Mouse.

"Listen," said Rabbit.
"I can hear a noise . . .
a **NOISY** noise . . .
a **HOOTY, HONKY**
noise.
It's getting **LOUDER**.
Can you hear it, Mouse?"

"Yes," she said.
"It must be the bus."

"No," shouted Rabbit.
"It's too loud."

honk
honk

hoot
hoot

honk
honk

"Wow, look up there! Geese!"

"What a racket," yelled Mouse.
"I can't hear myself think."

honk
honk

hoot
hoot

Rabbit and Mouse watched the geese.
They flew over their heads and far away.

"Where's our bus?" said Mouse. "It's getting hot."

"Let's go for a paddle in that splishy, splashy stream," said Rabbit. She hopped away from the bus stop.

"Wait!" cried Mouse.
"The bus will be here in a minute.
Mind you, the water looks lovely and cool."

Rabbit and Mouse

paddled in the stream.

Then they went back
to the bus stop.

"Where's our bus?"
said Mouse.
"We've been here AGES."

"My legs hurt," said Rabbit.
"I'm going to lie down
in that swishy-wishy grass."
She wandered away
from the bus stop.

"The bus might come," called Mouse.
"Mind you, I could do with
a lie-down myself."

Rabbit and Mouse lay down and had a rest.

Then they went back
to the bus stop.

"Where's our bus?"
said Mouse.
"It's never going to come."

"Look," cried Rabbit.
"Lookity-look.
The bus, the bus.
It's coming!"

"But it's coming
the wrong way,"
said Mouse.

The bus stopped and out
jumped Duck.
"There you are," she said.
"Got tired of waiting. Brought our tea."

"Oooo, yum!" said Rabbit and Mouse.

They sat in
the sunshine
and had a picnic.

Munchy carrot cake for Rabbit.
Crunchy cheese fritters for Mouse
and scrunchy worm waffles for Duck.

"That was scrummy," said Rabbit and Mouse.
"We'll see you onto the bus, Duck."

They went back
to the bus stop.
"Where's our bus?"
said Mouse.
"It's getting dark."

"Come back with us, Duck,"
said Rabbit.
"You can stay the night."

"OK," said Duck.
And they all went back
to Rabbit and Mouse's.

"Do you know," said Rabbit and Mouse to Duck.
"Not ONE bus came our way all day long."